£3.75

Write your name on the dotted line and stick a photograph of yourself on the WANTED poster.

Annual 1988

the Shoe People™

Illustrated by Rob Lee

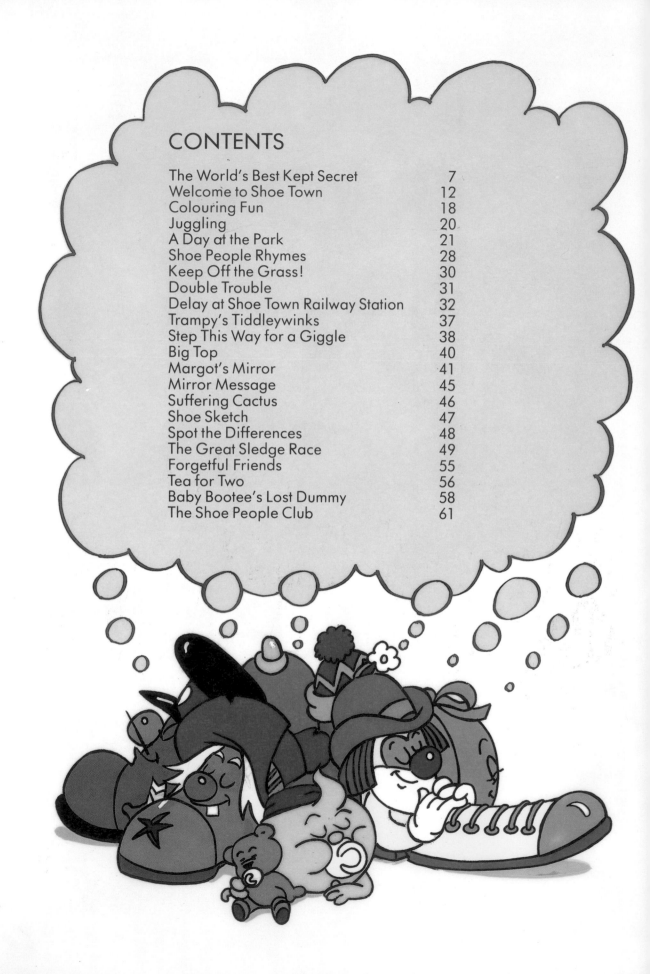

CONTENTS

THE WORLD'S BEST KEPT SECRET

In one of the back streets not too far from here is a very old shop that belongs to a shoe mender. The window is very dirty because the shoe mender doesn't bother to clean it. There's a curtain inside the window that's full of holes. The shop is very run-down and could really do with painting and smartening up.

The front room of the shop has a counter and behind the counter there are lots of tools. These are the tools that the shoe mender uses to repair shoes and boots.

There are many shelves around the room filled with repaired shoes and boots that are waiting to be collected by their owners. Each shoe and boot has been carefully labelled with the name and address of the owner.

There's a bell hanging above the front door inside the shop and when the door opens the bell rings telling the shoe mender that another customer has arrived!

"Good morning, madam, can I help you?" asks the shoe mender.

"Oh yes please, I have one of my husband's boots that he uses for gardening. Can you repair it? I'm afraid there's a big hole in the toe and another in the sole but I'm sure you will be able to mend it."

The shoe mender examines the boot carefully but there is nothing he can do to repair it.

"I'm so sorry but this boot is too badly worn for me to be able to repair it," says the shoe mender.

"Don't worry, I thought you might say that," says the lady. "I'll take it back home and throw it away."

"Well, madam," says the shoe mender, "perhaps I can dispose of it for you."

"Oh yes please, if you could," says the lady. The door closes behind the lady as she leaves the shop. The shoe mender moves the boot round the counter, looking at it carefully and saying, "You have become worn-out because they have never bothered to look after you. Once, when you were new, they would never have said, 'Just throw it away'. Never mind, I will polish your leather and make you look smarter and then you can stay in the BACK ROOM of the shop."

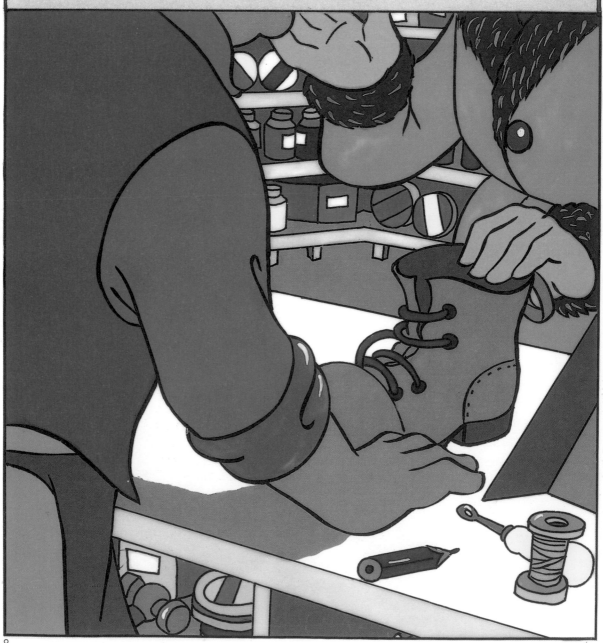

The shoe mender loves all shoes and boots so much that he can never throw them away. Over the years he has collected many worn out shoes and boots. There were other shoes and boots that he repaired but their owners forgot to collect and he keeps these as well.

In the back of his shop he has a room where all these shoes and boots are kept. The room is very dusty and there are lots of cobwebs. The floor is covered with boxes and tea chests. There are lots of shelves and cupboards. The boxes, tea chests, shelves and cupboards are full of shoes and boots. Many have been here for years. This back room has a very special SECRET and only one person knows it. Can you guess who that person could be?

No, it's not the shoe mender. The only person who knows the secret is me!

Can you keep a secret? Can you? Promise? Very well then, I will tell you the world's best kept secret.

When the shoe mender locks up every night to go home he makes sure that the door leading to the back is firmly closed. The door is so old that it doesn't shut very easily so the shoe mender has to slam it very hard. As the door slams shut the strangest thing happens.

A large cloud of dust fills the room and it's impossible to see anything in the room at all. As the dust settles one very worn-out boot comes to life and tells the rest of the shoes and boots that the time has come for more stories and adventures.

The back wall of the room completely disappears and we suddenly find ourselves in a beautiful town set in the countryside. This is Shoe Town where all the shoes and boots live. This is their magic world, a world where shoes and boots become real, just like you and me.

As you read through this book you will meet many of The Shoe People and even join in some of their games. Remember that you are now a friend of The Shoe People because, just like me, you know THE SECRET.

WELCOME TO SHOE TOWN

There is a long steep hill that leads into Shoe Town. It is called Toecap Hill, and if you stand on the top of the hill you can see all the houses in Shoe Town. P.C. Boot always starts his beat by walking down Toecap Hill into Shoe Town.

The first street he comes to is Shoe Street and there are some very unusual houses in this street. On the corner of Shoe Street is a house that looks like a circus tent. In fact a very funny clown lives here. His name is Charlie and he calls his house The Little Big Top. Charlie also performs lots of magic tricks. P.C. Boot never knows what colour The Little Big Top is going to be because Charlie likes to change the colour quite often and he does this by magic. Here's Charlie now, juggling three balls as usual.

"Good morning, Charlie," says P.C. Boot.

"Hello, P.C. Boot, lovely day isn't it?" says Charlie. "It's so nice today that I think I'll change The Little Big Top from blue to yellow with stars."

Charlie takes out his magic wand and to P.C. Boot's amazement there's a big flash and suddenly The Little Big Top is a completely different colour.

"Charlie, you are the cleverest clown in the whole world," says P.C. Boot.

The house next door to Charlie belongs to Trampy. It is called Tumbledown House and, as you can no doubt guess, it is not the smartest house in Shoe Town. Tumbledown House hasn't been painted for years. There are windows broken and even the chimney looks as though it might fall down at any time. Some of the tiles are missing from the roof but Trampy doesn't attach much importance to houses. There's Trampy in the garden watering the wild flowers.

"Good morning, Trampy, nice day to cut the lawn," says P.C. Boot with a smile.

"Cut the lawn and chop all these beautiful wild flowers

down! I would rather be locked up in Shoe Street Police Station than do such a terrible thing," laughs Trampy.

P.C. Boot can hear the noise of a lawnmower coming from the next garden. The mower seems to stop quite often and a very loud voice says, "SPOT ON, EXACTLY RIGHT." P.C. Boot looks over the fence and sure enough Sergeant Major is cutting his lawn.

Sergeant Major has the best kept lawn in Shoe Town. He always mows it in stripes and measures the width of every stripe with a ruler to make sure the measurement is exactly the same on each one.

"Hello, Sergeant Major, you're looking very busy today. I must say that Drill Hall certainly has the best kept lawn in Shoe Town," says P.C. Boot.

"THANK YOU, P.C. BOOT. CAN'T STOP. LOOKS LIKE RAIN IN THE AIR," says Sergeant Major in his very loud voice.

Swan Lake Cottage is the next house that P.C. Boot comes to. This is a very pretty thatched cottage that belongs to Margot the ballerina. Margot is in the front garden playing with Baby Bootee. Margot is rolling a large beach ball towards Baby Bootee, who will then hit the ball back to Margot. They are both laughing so much that they don't see P.C. Boot go by.

"Won't disturb them when they're having such a good time," says P.C. Boot to himself.

A few spots of rain appear on the footpath as P.C. Boot makes his way back to Shoe Street Police Station. Looks like Sergeant Major was right, P.C. Boot thinks to himself. It starts to rain faster and P.C. Boot decides to hurry back to the Police Station.

As he passes Puddle Villa he sees Wellington standing underneath the guttering of the house, getting absolutely soaked. Wellington just loves rainy days and has made holes along the guttering so that the water can pour out of the holes all over him.

"You'll catch your death of cold, my lad," says P.C. Boot as he rushes past.

"P.C. Boot, I'm Wellington and Wellingtons never get colds. We just love being wet," laughs Wellington, getting wetter and wetter.

P.C. Boot is soon back at Shoe Street Police Station. He takes his policeman's helmet off and hangs it by the door. He sits behind his desk and takes out his notebook to make a record of the day's events. He usually finishes with the same words every day.

All quiet in Shoe Town. P.C. Boot.

COLOURING FUN

Colour this picture of Trampy using the picture (left) as a guide.

JUGGLING

How many plates is Charlie juggling? The initials of the objects below will give you the answer.

the Shoe People ™

A DAY AT THE PARK

Some of the Shoe People had gone to the park for the day. Trampy and Wellington made straight for the slide. "Wheee!" cried Trampy as he whizzed down the slide at high speed.

P.C. Boot and Baby Bootee meanwhile were playing on the see-saw. It wasn't too easy though because P.C. Boot was heavier than Baby Bootee and she kept bouncing high in the air.

After a while some of the Shoe People decided to have a nap. Charlie the clown wasn't tired at all however and he soon became bored. "This isn't much fun," he sighed.

"I know!" he suddenly exclaimed. "I'll practise some of my tricks." "THAT'S ALL I NEED!" bellowed Sergeant Major. "Once you start practising your tricks I'll never get any sleep. I'M OFF!"

Sergeant Major marched off in a huff. "What that clown needs is some good old-fashioned drill," muttered Sergeant Major as he settled beneath an apple tree. "That would soon tire him out!"

Meanwhile, Charlie was entertaining the Shoe People by performing his animal impressions. "This is a donkey," said Charlie. "Cock-a-doodle-do! And this is an elephant. Tweety-Tweet-Tweet!"

The Shoe People laughed and laughed. "I'll now perform my balloon act for your entertainment," called Charlie. He began puffing up the balloon until it became very large.

Eventually the balloon was large enough. "Be careful it doesn't burst," cried Wellington. "Don't worry," replied Charlie as he tied a knot on the balloon and began floating slowly upwards.

As soon as he was well off the ground, Charlie decided to loop the loop. Up and over he went. "Make sure you don't get dizzy," called Margot. "I won't," laughed Charlie.

"Hold on tight," called P.C. Boot as Charlie let a little air out of the balloon and began flying through the sky at high speed. "Wheee!" cried Charlie, thoroughly enjoying himself.

Charlie zoomed to and fro high over trees and hills until he slowly floated down towards the Shoe People. "Marvellous!" called Wellington. "Encore!" cried Trampy and P.C. Boot.

"For my next trick I'll make my balloon disappear," chuckled Charlie. "How will you do that?" asked P.C. Boot. "Watch closely," said Charlie as he produced a sharp pin. Trampy covered his ears.

Sergeant Major had settled down and was snoozing peacefully, dreaming that all the Shoe People were marching neatly in step with their toe caps shining brightly, even Trampy's.

Nearby, Charlie was about to finish his act. "I like to end my performance with a bang," he chuckled as he stabbed the pin into the big balloon. The balloon burst with a huge BANG!

The noise was so loud that it woke Sergeant Major with such a fright that he jumped high in the air . . . right into the tree. "EEK! dive for cover," he cried. "MAN YOUR POSTS."

"KEEP CALM!" roared Sergeant Major, not really sure what to do except hold on tightly to the branch he was hanging from. Eventually the branch began creaking and suddenly it snapped.

The branch fell to earth with Sergeant Major still hanging on to it. Sergeant Major landed with a bump. Suddenly all the apples fell out of the tree landing on his head, BUMP! BUMPITTY-BUMP!

The apples kept falling until they almost completely covered Sergeant Major. "It's r-raining apples!" he groaned as he struggled to free himself. Just then the rest of the Shoe People arrived.

"Are you all right, Sergeant Major?" asked a concerned Margot as she helped remove the apples. "AHEM! It takes more than a few pippins to worry a good soldier," he replied crossly.

Just then Charlie arrived on the scene. "I hope I didn't frighten you when I burst my balloon," said Charlie. "Frightened? FRIGHTENED?" bellowed Sergeant Major. "NOT LIKELY!"

Charlie thought Sergeant Major was getting a bit hot and bothered so he saved the last part of his act for him . . . a cool jet of water from his trick flower. "WHY . . . !" began Sergeant Major.

"YOU STUPID CLOWN!" "Now, now," said Trampy quietly. "There's no need to be upset. After all, Charlie did give us a good show." "Oh well," said Sergeant Major, "I suppose you're right."

"But I thought you were asleep all the way through Charlie's act," chuckled Margot. "Well, ahem . . . yes I was," stuttered Sergeant Major. WE BELIEVE HIM, DON'T WE READERS . . . ?

THE SHOE PEOPLE ATE LOTS OF APPLES BEFORE GOING BACK TO PLAYING ON THE SWINGS AND SLIDES, BUT FIRST THEY LEFT SEVEN APPLES IN THIS PICTURE FOR YOU TO FIND. CAN YOU SPOT THEM?

SHOE PEOPLE RHYMES

copie pomes out. my garden

TRAMPY

I love wild flowers,
I love the trees,
I even love the buzzing bees.
When you see my house,
Please don't frown,
Because I love it,
Being Tumbledown!

MARGOT

my house

Swan Lake Cottage is so neat,
I think it's the prettiest house
    in Shoe Street,
The Shoe People come when they
    get the chance,
To see my lovely ballet dance!

Jamie

WELLINGTON

Muddy puddles are my
    favourite treat,
I splash in and out of them
    in Shoe Street.
I love the rain and when
    it pours,
You'll never find ME,
    sitting indoors.

CHARLIE

Cymon

I can float so very high,
On a red balloon up in the sky,
Sometimes though when I come down,
Sgt Major calls me a stupid clown.

SERGEANT MAJOR *MOTHER*

Sometimes Charlie gets me down,
Because he's such a stupid clown,
The Shoe People say I always shout,
I suppose I do when he's about.

P.C. BOOT *Father*

I love to go out on my
    beat,
And talk to my friends in
    Shoe Street,
We're never sad we never
    frown,
In our magic world of
    Shoe Town.

Help Wellington reach the pond without treading on a ladybird or stepping on the grass.

KEEP OFF THE GRASS

DOUBLE TROUBLE

Two of these ladybirds are identical. Can you help Wellington spot them?

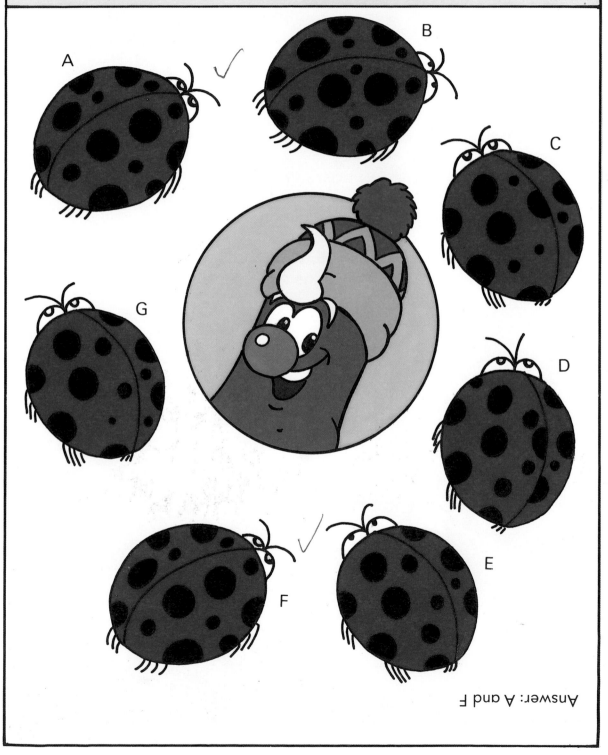

31

DELAY AT SHOE TOWN RAILWAY STATION

P.C. Boot was just finishing his lunch at Shoe Street Police Station when the telephone started to ring.

"Shoe Street Police Station, P.C. Boot speaking. Can I help you?" he said.

"P.C. Boot, thank heavens you're in. It's Mr Potter, the station master speaking. I have a terrible problem!" said a very panicked station master.

"Please calm down, Mr Potter, and tell me your trouble," said P.C. Boot.

"I have a train full of passengers going for a day's outing but a tree has fallen across the tracks completely blocking the railway line. What can I do?" said Mr Potter, very upset.

"Don't worry, Mr Potter, this sounds like a job for Sergeant Major. I will be at the railway station in ten minutes," said P.C. Boot.

P.C. Boot hurriedly made off for Drill Hall. Sergeant Major was marching up and down in his garden when P.C. Boot arrived. P.C. Boot quickly explained the problem of the fallen tree to Sergeant Major and asked for his help.

Sergeant Major went into Drill Hall and came back carrying a large rope over his shoulder. They both set out for Shoe Town Railway Station.

When they arrived at the railway station some of the Shoe People were standing on the platform. There was Margot, Baby Bootee, Sid Slipper and Trampy standing near the engine looking at the large tree blocking the line.

The rest of the Shoe People were sitting patiently in their carriages waiting for the obstacle to be removed.

Sergeant Major began to tie the rope round the tree. He knotted the rope in several places and finally tied the rope to the engine.

"EVERYONE STAND CLEAR!" he ordered. Sergeant Major turned to the engine driver and shouted, "PUT THE ENGINE IN REVERSE AND GO VERY SLOWLY."

The engine pulled and pulled but the tree was too big. It wouldn't move. "It's hopeless," said the engine driver. "The tree is far too heavy for my engine to pull. It would take an elephant to move that tree!"

"An elephant," said Charlie, standing on the platform watching what was going on. "That gives me an idea," he said and very quickly went out of the station.

Mr Potter, the station master, went along the platform telling the passengers in the carriages that it looked as if the trip would have to be cancelled. They were very disappointed. Some of them began to get off the train.

The engine driver was just about to turn the engine off and stop the steam coming out of the engine's funnel when a very strange loud noise could be heard.

BUMP! BUMP! BUMP! BUMP! It seemed to be coming from the front of the station master's office.

BUMP! BUMP! BUMP! BUMP! Just then, to everyone's surprise, a huge elephant appeared at the level crossing gate carrying Charlie on its back.

"Hello, everybody," said Charlie. "I've been to Shoe Town Zoo and asked if Bertha could come and help to remove the tree blocking the track."

Mr Potter opened the gate allowing Bertha on to the track. Sergeant Major held her trunk and took her towards the tree. Bertha stopped by the tree and turned her head towards Charlie who was still sitting on her back.

"Okay, Bertha," said Charlie. "Put your trunk around the tree and lift it clear of the railway line."

Mr Potter told everyone to stand back and keep clear and he held his red flag in the air making sure everyone was behind him.

Bertha wrapped her long trunk around the tree and very slowly, but very easily, lifted it clear of the tracks.

"Well done, Bertha, marvellous!" shouted Charlie somersaulting off her back.

The Shoe People cheered and cheered. Margot took a big cream cake out of her picnic basket and gave it to Bertha.

Bertha smiled as she ate it. Mr Potter got everyone back on the train and blew his whistle. The train pulled out of the station.

P.C. Boot and Sergeant Major took Bertha back to Shoe Town Zoo.

"Charlie does come up with a good idea sometimes," said P.C. Boot winking at Sergeant Major.

TRAMPY'S TIDDLEYWINKS

Trampy has made a game of tiddleywinks. Whoever gets a button into each of the objects wins the mystery prize. Make a tiddleywink game up for yourself. Join the dots to find some fabulous mystery prizes.

STEP THIS WAY FOR A GIGGLE

Wellington "Why are tall people lazier than short people?"
Trampy "I don't know. Why are tall people lazier than short people?"
Wellington "'Cos they're longer in bed!"

Charlie "Trampy, what has a green and yellow striped body, six hairy legs and big red eyes on stalks?"
Trampy "I don't know. Why do you ask?"
Charlie "One's just crawled into your hat!"

Margot "Why did the mother kangaroo scold her children?"
Wellington "I don't know why."
Margot "Because they ate biscuits in bed!"

Sgt Major "What's the noisiest of all sports?"
P.C. Boot "Motor racing?"
Sgt Major "No, tennis. Because you can't play it without raising a racket!"

Trampy "I've got a dog."
P.C. Boot "What do you call him?"
Trampy "Camera!"
P.C. Boot "Why?"
Trampy "'Cos he's always snapping!"

Trampy "What has four legs and one foot?"
Charlie "Tell me."
Trampy "A bed!"

Charlie "What did the balloon say to the pin?"
Sgt Major "I haven't a clue."
Charlie "Hi, Buster!"

Baby Bootee "What's the longest night of the year?"
Margot "I don't know."
Baby Bootee "A fortnight!"

Marshal Boot "When I was in Texas I used to chase cattle on horseback."
Charlie "Fancy that! I didn't know cattle could ride horses!"

P.C. Boot "What kind of invention was the clock?"
Sgt Major "I give in."
P.C. Boot "A timely one!"

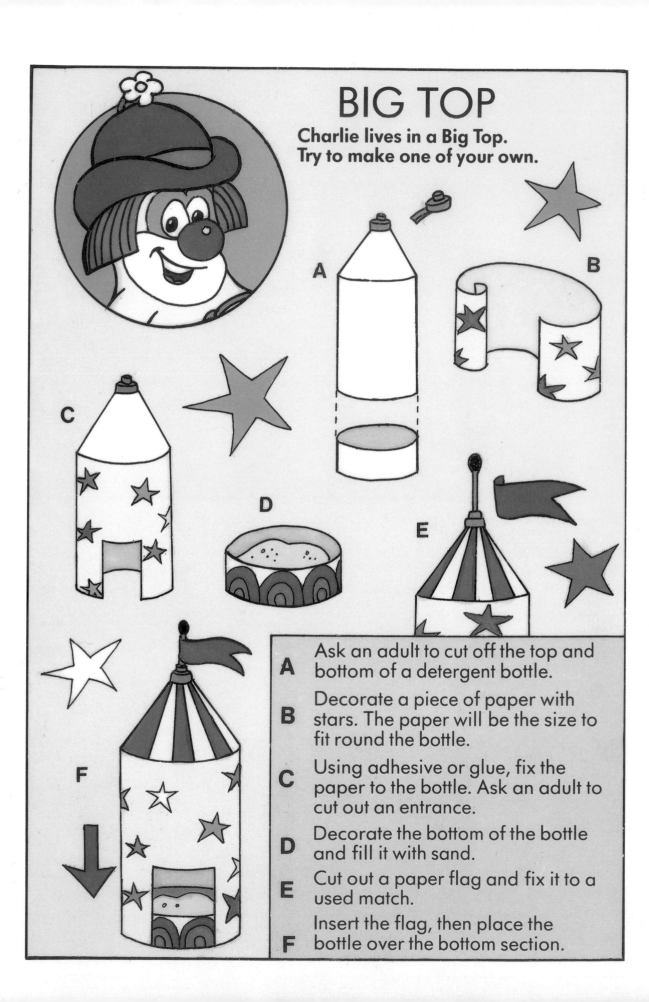

BIG TOP

**Charlie lives in a Big Top.
Try to make one of your own.**

A

B

C

D

E

F

A	Ask an adult to cut off the top and bottom of a detergent bottle.
B	Decorate a piece of paper with stars. The paper will be the size to fit round the bottle.
C	Using adhesive or glue, fix the paper to the bottle. Ask an adult to cut out an entrance.
D	Decorate the bottom of the bottle and fill it with sand.
E	Cut out a paper flag and fix it to a used match.
F	Insert the flag, then place the bottle over the bottom section.

MARGOT'S MIRROR

As usual it was a peaceful day at Shoe Town Police Station. P.C. Boot was settling down to his mid-morning cuppa. Nobody did anything wrong in Shoe Town so P.C. Boot had quite a quiet life.

P.C. Boot was quietly sipping his tea when he glanced out of the window. "Well I'll be blowed!" he cried, as he saw cups and saucers flying past the window. "I must be seeing things."

Meanwhile, across Shoe Street, Trampy was in the front garden of Tumbledown House tending his garden. Trampy liked his garden overgrown and wild so he didn't do very much tending.

41

Trampy looked over a bush to see a strange sight before his eyes. "I've heard of flying saucers but not flying *cups* and saucers!" exclaimed Trampy, as the cups and saucers went round in circles.

Trampy parted the leaves of the bush and peered over into the street. "So that explains it," he laughed. "It's just Charlie juggling." "Morning, Trampy," called Charlie as he passed by.

"I'm trying to break my record for juggling without dropping anything," chuckled Charlie. "I've lasted two hours already." "Good luck!" called Trampy as Charlie headed down Shoe Street.

Charlie decided to call on Margot. So he went up the garden path to Swan Lake Cottage. Margot's garden was full of roses and beautiful flowers in every colour of the rainbow.

Charlie tapped on the door with his toe so he could keep on juggling. There was no answer so Charlie, seeing that the door wasn't locked, stepped inside and immediately tripped over the carpet.

"Oh no!" cried Charlie as the cups and saucers flew through the air and crashed into Margot's mirror. The cups and saucers broke and so did the mirror. "Oh my goodness!" moaned Charlie.

"Instead of breaking a record I broke a mirror," groaned Charlie as he headed back to his tent. "I seem to remember having an old mirror at one time," he muttered as he searched around.

Charlie found his mirror and dashed up to Margot's cottage and replaced it before Margot returned. When Margot came back from shopping, she said, "I think I'll practise my ballet."

Margot was just about to go into a spin when she looked in the mirror. "Eek!" she cried. "I've become *FAT*!" Margot blinked in disbelief at the sight before her. "I'm as big as an elephant!" she wailed.

Just then Charlie arrived. "It's not you," he explained, "I broke your mirror and the only other one I could find was an old fairground mirror." "So that's it," said Margot in relief.

"Don't worry," said Charlie, "I'll get you a brand new one." "Not just yet," laughed Margot. "We can have lots of fun with this one first." All the Shoe People came around to look into the old fairground mirror. "I'm all wobbly-looking!" smiled Wellington. "I look like a jelly!" chuckled P.C. Boot. "This is even more fun than juggling," laughed Charlie. "And a lot safer too!" giggled Margot.

SUFFERING CACTUS

Help Marshal Boot get to the building without touching a prickly cactus.

SHOE SKETCH

Copy Wellington and Margot into the grid below.

SPOT THE DIFFERENCES

Can you spot TEN differences between the pictures?

THE GREAT SLEDGE RACE

Snow had been falling all through the night and Shoe Town was completely covered in a beautiful white snow blanket. The green fir trees looked so pretty with snow sticking to their branches. Scenes like these made everyone think of Christmas.

The Shoe People had gathered in the park. They had taken their sledges and were very slowly making their way up the hill. The sledges were of different shapes and sizes.

Trampy hadn't really got a sledge at all. He had taken a door off his cupboard in the kitchen and tied some string around the handle. This was what he was pulling behind him.

Sergeant Major had the best sledge. His was made out of metal with runners that were shaped like tracks on an army tank but completely smooth. It was painted in army green and lightly polished.

Charlie didn't have a sledge at all. Instead he pulled Margot's sledge up the hill while Margot and Baby Bootee sat on it. Margot had a red plastic sledge with a seat on the back.

P.C. Boot was carrying a large tea tray and Wellington pulled something that looked like a small boat. They all reached the top of the hill.

"GATHER ROUND EVERYONE," said Sergeant Major. "WE ARE GOING TO HAVE A RACE."

"Oh great!" said Charlie.

"STUPID CLOWN!" said Sergeant Major. "YOU CAN'T JOIN IN. HOW CAN YOU ENTER A SLEDGE RACE WITHOUT A SLEDGE?"

"Well I'm so long that I can just ski down the hill," said Charlie.

They all lined up at the top of the hill. Trampy sat on his cupboard door and next to him were Margot and Baby Bootee on the red plastic sledge. Then there was Charlie just standing there. Next, Sergeant Major on his army sledge, P.C. Boot sitting on his tea tray, and Wellington in the boat sledge.

"ATTEN-SHUN!" shouted Sergeant Major. "AFTER THREE THE RACE WILL START. ONE . . . TWO . . . THREE. WE'RE OFF!"

The race began. Sergeant Major went straight into the lead, followed closely by P.C. Boot on his tea tray.

Trampy's door had turned round in the snow and Trampy was coming down the hill backwards. He was being followed by Margot and Baby Bootee. Baby Bootee was covering her eyes.

Wellington's boat sledge had overturned and he was going over and over in the snow.

"This is absolutely great," he was shouting.

Charlie was still standing at the starting point and hadn't moved.

"Come on, Charlie," shouted Trampy. "You'll be last."
Charlie started to ski along the snow. He was going faster and faster. He soon passed Trampy who was still going backwards. He was catching up with P.C. Boot but Sergeant Major was still in the lead. Wellington was out of the race altogether. He had rolled over and over and looked more like a giant snowball now.

Charlie came to a slight bump in the ground and as he hit it he lifted high into the air just like a ski jumper. He somersaulted twice in mid-air and landed on the finishing line just ahead of Sergeant Major.

Sergeant Major crossed the finish line and got off his sledge. He looked quite angry as he walked over to Charlie. The others crossed the finish line one after another. Trampy crossed it still travelling backwards. They all gathered round Charlie, but before anyone could say anything, Charlie said, "A marvellous sledge race and I declare the sledge race champion of Shoe Town to be Sergeant Major."

"ME?" said Sergeant Major. "BUT YOU WERE FIRST, CHARLIE."

"No, Sergeant Major. I can't be the sledge race champion when I didn't use a sledge," said Charlie.

The Shoe People cheered the new champion. Sergeant Major took a bow and said, "RIGHT. LET'S ALL GO BACK TO DRILL HALL. I HAVE SOME·HOT ARMY SOUP COOKING. THAT WILL WARM US UP."

"Great idea," said Charlie. And they all set out for Drill Hall.

FORGETFUL FRIENDS

Trampy's friends have left some things behind. There are two hats, balloons, a truncheon, a dummy and a rose. Who do they belong to?

TEA FOR TWO

Go to tea with Trampy by using a dice and counters. Throw a six to start. If you land on a red square – miss a go. If you land on a green square – go forward two places. If you land on a dark blue square – go back one place.

4

3

2

START 1

5 Lift off with Charlie and floa to 8.

23   24   25   26

22 Hitch a lift in Charlie's car. Spring to 24.

FI

37

21   20   18

19 Wellington splashes you – miss a turn to dry off.

6   7   8

29

30

31

28

32

9
Help Margot
pick up her
shopping.
Miss a turn.

10

11

7

33

12

13

36   35   34

16 Borrow Baby
Bootee's skateboard.
Go forward to 20.

17   15

14 Sgt Major parades
the troops across
your path.
Go back to 12.

BABY BOOTEE'S LOST DUMMY

It was a lovely day in Shoe Town. Baby Bootee asked Margot if she could play in Shoe Town woods. The ballerina said yes, providing Baby Bootee was back in time for tea.

Baby Bootee was having so much fun that she didn't realise the time. "I'd better get home or I'll be late for tea," she cried. As she raced home, she realised she'd left her dummy behind.

Baby Bootee dashed back to the woods and searched everywhere. "I can't for the life of me remember where I left it," she muttered as she left no stone unturned.

After scurrying to and fro for what seemed ages, Baby Bootee decided to stop for a rest. "ULP! I think I'm lost," she gulped. "And it's g-getting dark." Baby Bootee looked around nervously.

"How will I find my way home now?" wondered Baby Bootee. Just then she saw something coming towards her from deep in the woods. "Wh-what's that?" gulped Baby Bootee nervously.

Baby Bootee cowered against a tree as the light became brighter and brighter. Soon it was so close she could almost touch it. "I hope it's f-friendly," she said, wishing P.C. Boot was there to help her.

"Now what on earth are you doing in the woods so late?" boomed a very loud voice. "THANK GOODNESS!" exclaimed Baby Bootee in relief. "It's just Maurice Miner boot."

THE SHOE PEOPLE CLUB

Join The 1988 Shoe People Club

Now you can become a member of THE SHOE PEOPLE CLUB and be a special friend of TRAMPY, MARGOT, P.C. BOOT, CHARLIE, SERGEANT MAJOR and everyone in Shoe Town.

Lots of new things are planned for club members this year with gifts, newsletters, things to do, competitions and much more besides.

ALL NEW FOR 1988! Everything in the 1988 club will be completely new and different from 1987. In your first pack you will receive:

* Your official 1988 MEMBERSHIP CERTIFICATE
* Your official MEMBERSHIP CARD
* A New CLUB BADGE
* A bright New POSTER
* A letter welcoming you to the club from P.C. Boot

AND

YOUR SPECIAL GIFT
THE SHOE PEOPLE PENCIL CASE

Ask Mum or Dad if you can join now.
Send a letter telling us:

Your Name
Address (including postcode)
Age
Date of Birth
PLEASE PRINT IN BLOCK CAPITALS

The letter MUST be signed by a Parent or Guardian.
Enclose a cheque or postal order for £3.50 made payable to "The Shoe People Club".

The address to write to is:
The Shoe People Club
School Drive
Amblecote
Stourbridge
West Midlands
DY8 4DQ